The Ghosts of Sherwood

ALSO BY CARRIE VAUGHN

The Ghosts of Sherwood

Carrie Vaughn

A TOM DOHERTY ASSOCIATES BOOK

NEW YORK

THE GHOSTS OF SHERWOOD

Copyright © 2020 by Carrie Vaughn

Cover art and design by Elizabeth Dresner

Edited by Lee Harris

A Tor.com Book
Published by Tom Doherty Associates
120 Broadway
New York, NY 10271

www.tor.com

Tor® is a registered trademark of
Macmillan Publishing Group, LLC.

ISBN 978-1-250-75210-9 (ebook)
ISBN 978-1-250-75211-6 (trade paperback)

First Edition: June 2020

For Errol and Olivia

The Ghosts of Sherwood

i

A MESSENGER ARRIVED TO say that the lord and lady of the manor would return that afternoon. Mary had a moment of panic. Her parents had been gone for months, nothing was ready, they would arrive to find the manor in a state of disaster and it would be her fault—But no, everything was fine. She had only to tell the kitchen that there'd be more to feed at supper, with them and all their retinue. Mother and Father had been off in Surrey to see the king—a deeply serious trip wrapped up in politics. Father had joked that he might really lose his head this time, laughing and winking like he always did no matter how serious things got. Mother hadn't laughed, not that time.

"Messenger's arrived," Mary said to the cook, who looked up from dough she was kneading. "The lord and lady will be home for supper."

Joan's face lit. "Oh, wonderful news!" Then her expression fell. "That's a dozen more for supper, at least, and anyone who's come back with them."

"We've got the extra geese; they're ready for butchering, I think," Mary said. "Or would the pig be better? It's early yet." They would need the pig smoked and made into sausages for winter, but perhaps it could be spared for this.

"There's good reasons for either of them," Joan said cautiously, which also meant, *You are the lady of the manor until your mother returns, it's your decision.*

Mary winced. She thought she was getting better at this but there was always something new to consider. "Mother would say to butcher the geese, wouldn't she?"

Joan smiled. "Yes, my lady."

"Then we'll do that."

"Very good."

Mary went on to the rest of the chores. Chambers needed airing, fresh rushes put down, more wood for the hearth brought in. The hall would be crowded tonight. The news spread fast; the whole place grew lively. Next was to see if her siblings were presentable. She found Eleanor sitting on the low paddock wall outside the main yard. She was looking out at the road, waiting.

"It'll be a few hours before they get here," Mary said. "You don't have to wait here all that time." The girl set her jaw, pursed her lips: she would wait. Her back was straight, her hands clasped. The hem of her kirtle was muddy, but that was all right; the rest of her was clean enough. Her light brown hair was a bit of a mess. "Can I braid your hair again?"

Eleanor hesitated, then nodded. Mary set to work untying her hair, quickly combing it out with her fingers, and braiding it up again, all neat and tidy.

"How's that?" Eleanor nodded once and turned her gaze back to the road, which would stay empty for hours yet, but that hardly mattered.

Mary had no idea where John was and decided he was old enough to take care of himself. And she . . . she suddenly wanted to be somewhere else.

"If you see John, don't tell him I've gone out," Mary told her sister, who rolled her eyes and let out an offended sigh. Of course she wouldn't tell John anything. Mary had only to avoid him.

Mary raced to the chambers she and Eleanor shared by the back way, where no one was likely to see her, and changed out of her kirtle and veil and into her tunic and leggings and sturdy leather shoes, shoved her hair under her cap and sneaked back out again. Fortunately, everyone was so busy they didn't notice. At the back of the yard, she took a moment to make sure John wasn't in sight. Then she ran, across the road and the meadow beyond, and then to the edge of Sherwood Forest.

When she dressed in a gown and wore her hair braided up and veiled as she ought, she looked like a woman grown. She had already had one offer of marriage, which her parents instantly refused—she was too young, they said, and the offer too grasping. Mary wasn't supposed to know about it, and she did not know what to think. Flattered or horrified, or both at once. But in her leggings and old tunic and cap, she looked younger than she was, a girl still allowed to run loose in the woods, to avoid thinking of things like whether she ought to be flattered or horrified by sudden marriage offers.

Soon, every bit of the manor was out of sight, and she was alone. Cool shadows closed in, and her chest filled with the scent of living wood and rotting leaves, the opposite of hearth and stable. The peace of it went to her bones. She walked, putting her hand on trunks, brushing fingertips against rough bark, stepping as lightly as she could on silk-soft, mossy earth.

She came to the tree she sought, an ancient oak with a bloated trunk and branches that twisted and reached, shading everything around it until nothing else grew. A good oak for climbing. With a jump, she grabbed the lowest branch, swung up, then climbed, shimmying up the trunk to the next branch, lifting herself to the one after, until she came to the well-known lookout. The forest thinned enough here that from this position she could see far down the road that led to the manor. This was one of the trees where outlaws once stood watch and laid ambushes. Once, this forest had been so haunted that even well-armed men would not travel there. That had been a long time ago. No more outlaws haunted Sherwood. So everyone said.

"What do you see? My eyes aren't so good these days."

Mary flinched but kept her footing on the solid bough and her hold on the branch above her. The question came from a hooded figure standing in the branches of the next tree over. Staff tucked under one arm, he leaned up against the trunk and kept himself hidden in shadow.

The ghost of the forest had spoken to her before, always like this, creeping out of nowhere as if he'd been spying on her. The first time he'd done so was the first time she'd come to Sherwood by herself when she was ten, sneaking out just to see if she could, terrified she'd lose her way, thrilled to be alone with the quiet and vastness of it all. A voice had come out of the trees just like this, and she'd screamed and run until she realized that all he'd said was "Hello there." He never got any closer than this. Never let her see him full in the light. He had a beard, she thought. He might have been just a man, lurking deep in the woods for reasons of his own.

Or he might have been a ghost.

"Some dust far off but getting closer," she answered.

"A large party, then?"

"The lord and lady never travel with too large a party. Likely they're traveling fast." The lord and lady preferred traveling lightly and at speed, from long habit.

"Returning from meeting the king, yes?"

She took her eyes away from the road a moment, but no, he was still hidden, the shape of a man with no detail revealed. She wondered how he knew, how the gossip of the manor reached him here. Or if he simply *knew*. "Yes."

The dust grew, resolved itself into riders. No litters and wagons for her parents and their train—the wagon with their tents and supplies would follow more slowly. Their pace was calm. She could make out the rippling, rose-colored fabric of her mother's skirt, draped along her horse's flank.

"Can you tell how the mood is from here? How the journey went?"

"I won't know how it went until I see Father's face," she said.

"And see if he smiles or frowns?"

"No. And see if his smile is glad or wicked." Her father would be smiling in any case.

The ghost laughed. "I know that wicked smile. Good luck, then."

He faded back to the oak's shadows and made not a sound. No leaves rustled. There was no smack on the dirt as he dropped to the ground. He might have melted into bark. Not a man at all, then. Except that this was Sherwood and she knew what was possible.

She tried for quiet as she climbed out of her own tree, sliding from bough to bough, leaning against the trunk, dropping to soft earth with bent knees. Mostly, she succeeded, but not as well as the ghost.

Mary of Locksley ran for home to be there when her parents arrived.

SOME DAYS PRIOR...

ON ONE OF THE best days of Marian's life, King Richard gave his blessing to her and Robin's marriage, and brought down his corrupt brother John. On one of the worst, they received news that King Richard had died, that same brother would be crowned as his heir, and Robin decided he had no choice but to swear fealty to a man he hated.

This day was neither best nor worst. No one was in danger of being hanged, so that was good. Robin's most recent campaign against the king had been successful; he'd gotten the charter he wanted to protect the rights of landholders in England. But this had all become most uncomfortable, the barons who had rebelled and those who had stayed loyal camped on the same plain, eyeing each other with their packs of retinue and too many weapons at hand.

Still, Marian would not have missed seeing the look on the king's face for anything, when her husband said straight out to him, "Sire, when good people become outlaws, perhaps it is time to change the laws. As you well know." Robin had gotten nearly everything he'd wanted. He would never lose his holding out of royal spite again. He'd been about to demand an apology on top of everything, when Marian gave him a quelling look across the room, and, at last, Robin fell silent.

Now she only wanted to be home. She had never been away from the children for so long. Time was, she couldn't have imagined wanting home and quiet, hearth and children. Time was, she couldn't have imagined growing old at all. And Robin . . . Robin was running out of battles to fight.

Right at this moment, she and Robin were about to face King John, and while nobody was threatening to hang anybody this time, she wished herself elsewhere.

The king, haughty and fine as ever, held court in his pavilion, and the barons came to pay their respects, to show that they were all friends now. This must have been very gratifying to him, especially when Marian and Robin came before him, polite as they could manage. A silence fell, everyone turning to watch. They all knew the stories, knew that every meeting between these two had ended with shouting, and sometimes with dead bodies. Marian donned the courtliest smile she had and curtseyed neatly. She squeezed Robin's fingers, where her hand rested over his, to remind him to bow. He did so, just enough. King John—and after sixteen years, it was still strange thinking that—was close to fifty and obviously tired. The throne he had coveted so much had worn him down. Ruling was more difficult than wanting, especially when your vassals had had enough of you. When Robin appeared before him, the king seemed to sigh, as if this was one chore he would rather do without. So at least they all agreed on that.

Robin, not so young himself anymore, glared daggers at the man. The Baron of Locksley had a dusting of gray in his light brown hair, but his smile was bright as ever. Bright and cutting like a knife edge. King John's gaze slipped away from Robin to rest on Marian, and he seemed relieved to let it.

"How very good to see you, Lady Marian," the king said. "It's been a long time, hasn't it?"

"It has, sire," she said.

"You have children, yes?"

"God has blessed us with three, all strong and healthy."

The king flashed a smile that might have been genuine—even he brightened at talk of children. He had five of his own, as well as a typically royal assortment of bastards. But then the smile turned sly.

"Are they as difficult to manage as your husband?"

The question stretched the limits of her diplomatic

skills. She said, very sweetly, "Happily, they are very much like my husband. No one will ever take advantage of them."

In the slight pause that followed, Marian wondered if she had undone all of the advantages Robin and the other barons had won here. But King John laughed.

"You were wasted on him, my dear." He looked Robin up and down in that calculating way he had. Marian put pressure on Robin's hand again. *Be quiet, for just another moment.*

"Sire," she murmured. And then they were dismissed, to let the next baron play out the niceties.

Out of sight of the royal pavilion, she wrapped her arm around Robin's and leaned into him, to let herself rest a moment. "You did well," she said. "I didn't have to gag you."

He laughed, and she was relieved the sound was genuine and not forced. Polite, forced laughter didn't suit Robin a bit.

"Just this once, he's right," her husband said as they walked on. "About you being wasted on me. You should have married a prince." His face was still refined despite the wrinkles at his eyes, a touch of gauntness at his cheeks. He'd grown more thoughtful, some of his starry brightness not dimmed, but turned inward.

"You think I would have been happy, doing this sort of

thing every day? I'm much happier with you." He raised her hand and kissed it.

She started back for their camp, but Robin turned a different way.

"What is it?" she asked.

"I've been speaking with Robert de Ros. I thought you should hear what he has to say."

Sir Robert de Ros, Baron of Helmsley, one of the rebels from the north, an ally of Robin's. "I thought the war was done." What mischief was he planning? Robin will *retire* from mischief, she vowed.

"This isn't about the war." Robin led her to a small encampment that had a celebratory air, streamers fluttering from tent poles, a musician playing lute. Marian found she wasn't in the mood for music or merriment.

"Locksley!" A polished middle-aged man called out and came over from the gathering in the camp. He was accompanied by a much younger man with a thin beard and careful manner. The young one kept glancing at the older, then at Robin and Marian with an astonished look that suggested he might flee at any moment. She'd seen that look before; Robin frequently inspired it. "My lady," Helmsley said, bowing cautiously, as if gauging an unknown horse's temperament.

"Good day, Sir Robert," she said.

"You did your duty to the king?" Robert de Ros said to

Robin, nodding off to the royal pavilion.

"I am not ashamed to say I kept my mouth shut and hid behind my wife's skirts. His Majesty was much more pleased to speak with Lady Marian, anyway."

Robert laughed, as he was meant to. "I'm glad you're here. I would very much like to present to you my eldest son, William. William, this is the Baron of Locksley and his Lady Marian. You might have heard of them."

William pulled himself together and managed a bow with some poise to it. "My lord, my lady, it's an honor, truly." He didn't even stammer. Perhaps there was some hope for him.

"Well met, young William," Robin said. "Your father let you in for any excitement this past year?"

"I suppose it depends on what you'd call excitement," William said, glancing at his father, shrugging as if he was afraid of giving the wrong answer. "Nothing like all the things you've done. I helped fortify the manor and held it for him while he went off to the war. Not so exciting, really. But it could have been."

"I'm very glad it wasn't. Good man."

The young man grinned happily at the praise and gave another quick bow.

Sir Robert turned calculating. "He is a good man. I think it would be a good match for both our families."

Marian froze, William blushed red. Robin had been

making deals, it seemed.

Robin said, "We'd like to keep Mary with us for another year or so. But yes, I'm sure we can come to an arrangement."

"Oh, of course, plenty of time to decide such things. But those of us in the north, we need to stick together, don't we?"

Would this be a political alliance, or was he looking for money? Or simply the name, to be able to claim family ties to Locksley? Who could say; William de Ros seemed pleasant enough. Marian liked that his manner was earnest and not arrogant. She reassured herself that no one would dare treat Mary poorly, for risk of angering her famous father.

"We will speak of this further in good time," Robin said.

"Indeed, indeed."

"Locksley!" another lord called out. "Will you shoot something for us? Show us what you can do!" The man was clearly in his cups, laughing too loudly, too tauntingly.

Robin stiffened before turning to smile at the man. The sly smile. "I beg your pardon, sir, but I don't seem to have a bow with me. This being a peaceful gathering."

"Use mine!" Helmsley's camp had all sorts of weapons,

including bows. The drunk lord stumbled to grab one from a rack.

"God save us from idiots," Robin muttered. "Alas, friend. I must decline. Doesn't seem quite the time or place for it."

Helmsley tried to make an end of it, stepping between them. "Now, there's plenty of food and drink for all. Let us raise a toast to the peace, shall we?"

But the taunting lord would not quit. "Perhaps you're not as great an archer as they say you are."

Twenty years earlier, Robin would have taken up the bow and shot the man's cap off. Marian felt him tense beside her. Gathering up his civility like scattered coins. For a moment, she had no idea what he was going to do.

He laughed and offered a mocking bow. "Perhaps not. You should ask the bards who sing about me, hm?" He turned to Helmsley and William. "Safe journey home, my friends. We'll speak again soon."

They bowed in turn and watched Robin and Marian go, walking back to their camp. Marian's thoughts had scattered utterly. Robin clung to her hand, his touch full of nerves and anger and more.

"Robin . . ." she started. She had a hundred things to say to him.

"What did you think of William de Ros? He seems a nice lad," he said, as if speaking of the weather.

"When were you going to tell me that you have arranged our eldest daughter's marriage?"

"Right now." He smiled, but it didn't win her over. "It is a good match. She'll be taken care of. Her children will have land and title. They get the association of our name. I like the boy's look."

"Will she like him?"

He hesitated, which he hardly ever did. "I think so. Marian, she'll have to fly the nest sometime—"

"I would rather she do it in her own time, in her own way. Like we did."

"You want some nice brave lad to come along and worship at her feet and win her love?"

She knew what a rare and precious thing she and Robin had won for themselves. Looking around, she saw no other husband and wife walking arm in arm, still gazing adoringly at each other after twenty years. One generally did not see husbands and wives together at all. That was only one of the reasons people stared after Robin and Marian. How uncomfortable it was, to have songs and stories told about their love. How lucky they were, to fall in love before they married, rather than hoping to fall in love after.

"And why not?" she said stubbornly.

"I'm trying to do what is best for her. She knows her duty—"

"What a thing to say! What if I had known my duty all those years ago?"

"Marian—"

"Little John was right; you've very nearly turned into what you once fought against so fiercely." She let go of his arm and marched off before she said something even worse.

"My lady—"

"When we return home, you will tell her about this yourself."

He winced. "I had hoped you would—"

"No."

"Don't you think it's really best for a mother—"

"No!" She put more distance between them, and he followed sullenly.

Time, Mary needed more time . . . no, in just two years, she'd be the age Marian was when she met Robin and he upended her world. Maybe a quiet arranged marriage would be better . . .

They and their retinue camped like they were under siege. Apart from everyone else, a defensible space of meadow between them and the next cluster of tents, men on guard. She had felt like they were being watched from the moment they arrived; she constantly looked over her shoulder.

Worst part of it was, she often found they *were* being

watched. And not even by the king's men. Everyone was watching Robin, to see what he would do. It wore her out, that she must act like nothing was wrong in the middle of it all.

Will greeted her almost as soon as she came in view. He was a tall man, solid, with well-worn hands and crow's-feet from so much watching and worrying. "Where's Robin?" He looked over her shoulder for her absent companion.

"We're arguing," Marian said darkly.

"Oh. Well. We have a visitor."

Enough, when would this all be enough, when could they go home . . . Robin came up beside them.

"What is it?" Looking around, he marked every person within his view. His left fist squeezed, holding a bow that wasn't there.

"Visitor," their old friend said, stepping aside to show where he had seated the man by their fire.

"Oh, dear," Robin said, looking on the Earl of Pembroke, Sir William Marshal.

The most famous knight in England, and perhaps in all of Europe, was an old man now but as impressive as ever. His thick white hair was tamed under a cap, his tabard was pristine, and his hand rested on his sword as easily as a songbird came to rest on a branch. He stood, and he was so very tall and broad. Age had not bent him a bit.

Marian glanced at Robin, wondering what he would do.

"My lord," Robin said, bowing his head. Marian had only ever seen him show this kind of deference to King Richard.

"My lord," Marshal replied, and offered his hand. They shook. "Well met."

"How may I serve you?" Robin seemed a bit stunned, as if he had missed the last stair.

Marshal's smile turned wry. "I only wish to give you my goodwill, sir. And to say I hope that this marks an end to all your talk and trouble."

"Ah. Yes. Just so. I hope so too. That will be up to our lord and king, won't it?"

"And he will be watching, I can assure you."

"Is that a threat?" Robin said, smiling as if to make a joke, but his gaze was hard.

"Only if you take it as one. I mean you no harm, Locksley. But do try to stay out of trouble for a while, yes?"

"Yes, sir."

The old knight turned to her. "My lady, your reputation for grace and beauty falls far short of your presence. You have my admiration." He bowed.

"My lord Pembroke, you are very kind." She gazed at him in wonder.

"Fare you well, friends." He bowed again and departed.

They watched him go.

"I think that man does charm better even than you, Robin," Will said.

"No doubt about it. God's wounds, I thought I was going to faint." He blew out a breath he must have been holding.

Marshal's retinue waited for him some distance off, and they included his eldest son, also William, a man of five-and-twenty who shared his father's height and strength if not his reputation. He had sided with the rebel barons—at first. Then he had repented. He'd been eager to display his loyalty since then. Robin didn't like the man much.

"And we will all watch each other," Robin murmured. The younger William Marshal kept glancing at them over his shoulder, long after the others had turned away.

"This charter will not last," Will said. "This peace will not last."

The Baron of Locksley had nothing to say to that.

"Robin, I want to go home," Marian said.

"And so we shall, my love. We'll leave at dawn."

MARIAN HAD NOT GROWN up in the north, in the shadow of the forests and the wilds of the moors. She had been raised in Norman courts, taught courtly graces and speech, learned to hold herself like an ornament, to flatter men of power. The north had seemed a wilderness then, full of outlaws and danger. But after twenty years, it had become home. The road from Surrey went past towns and villages, chapels large and small with pealing bells, market squares, pastures full of sheep, fields full of farmers. Then the villages and settlements gave way, the first of the twisted, ancient oaks appeared—far off on distant wild hillsides, like ghosts in a haze. Then closer, until their shadows touched the road itself and the air grew thick with the scent of the forest, old wood and rich earth, and the sunlight seemed to take on a green cast. This wilderness was home, and she was happy to return to it. When she was young, she couldn't imagine a life outside court, which seemed the center of the world. Now she was sure Robin had rescued her from something grim and stifling.

Finally, they arrived back home at Locksley, in the comforting shade of Sherwood Forest.

"All seems well," Will said, shading his eyes and surveying the manor, its lands, tenants in the fields and in their workshops. He kept sword and bow on his saddle, close to hand.

"Expecting to see it all burned down, were you?" Robin said.

He'd meant it as a joke, but Will's look was somber. "You have enemies. Especially now."

"What can they do to me now?"

Marian exchanged a serious glance with Will. Here they were, watching the man's back, just as they always had. The manor gates stood wide open, as they ought, and Marian sighed. She needn't have worried. She trusted the men and women they'd put in charge of the place—many of them had been with Robin in the old days.

Robin kept pressing Marian the whole trip. "You'll speak to Mary—"

"No, I will not. I will not defy you on this, but you must be the one to explain her duty to her." Marian was the last woman in England who would force her daughter to marry anyone she did not wish. Surely, Robin knew this.

The hero of Sherwood sighed, defeated.

Will worried about threats from without, but they entered the stable yard to find Mary and John shouting at each other. What a greeting, after so many months away.

"You went without me!" yelled John, their middle child, son and heir of the great Robin of Locksley. "You said I could go along next time you went to the forest!"

"I did not," Mary muttered, trying for dignity and only managing flushed and furious. She was scuffed and sweaty, wearing boy's clothes. She still had height on her younger brother, but probably not for much longer. "You want to go out to the woods, just go; don't make me carry you."

"I don't need to be carried!"

"Yes, every time we go to the woods, you get lost!"

"Which is why I *asked*—"

"I don't need to tell you whenever I go somewhere—"

"So, instead you sneak out like a thief—"

Well, that was a bit cutting.

"You're very tiresome, John," Mary said flippantly, which drove her brother to further rage.

"Now then, let's have a proper hello for your long-absent parents, shall we?" Robin said in a calculated interruption.

The pair managed to put on cheerful faces to greet the crowd of horses and riders coming in through the gate. Not so full of righteous independence that they were ready to turn outlaw. Not quite yet. Her two eldest were both lanky and awkward, growing too fast and struggling to stretch their wings. Especially Mary, who was by most counts a woman grown, but Marian blinked and still saw the child she'd been. They both had Marian's chestnut hair and Robin's rich brown eyes.

Hostlers and folk of the house came out to greet them, telling how things were and what had gone wrong in their absence. Marian smiled at the stableboy who took her horse's reins, and he blushed.

Mary and John came to her, offered a quick curtsey and bow in turn before she scooped them into an embrace and buried her face in their hair to take a deep breath of the smell of them, full of sweat and dust and life.

"You're both alive, good," she said. Mary had grown. They looked straight at each other, the same height. Marian suddenly wanted to cry, but instead she hugged them again and passed them on to greet their father. Mary wasn't ready to go off to be married, she *wasn't*.

Scanning the yard for her youngest, she found Eleanor, age eight, sitting on the steps to the main house and weaving straw into something intricate, apparently oblivious to the commotion. The girl was clean, her light hair braided and her kirtle neat and straight—muddy at the hem, but that only meant she'd been outside, which was good. Well fed, she even had some color in her cheeks. So, perhaps things at home had not gone entirely amiss while they were away.

Marian never wanted to leave home again. *This* was what she wanted now; *this* was what Robin had promised her, though he hadn't quite known it at the time.

"What are you two on about?" Robin asked his two eldest, hands on hips. He sounded far too amiable for his children to ever believe he was cross with them.

"Mary's been running off to Sherwood alone!" John announced.

"And you think you ought to have the duty of accompanying her?"

"Well, no! But you'd have words if I ever ran off alone!"

"Have you tried it?" Robin said, and John was taken aback.

"So, you don't care if I turn outlaw?"

Mary ranted, "I'm not turning outlaw! I just want some peace and quiet, away from *you*!"

Marian left them to it and went to the steps to sit by Eleanor. "Hello, sweetling."

The girl glanced up, then back to the work in her hands. She didn't say a word but shifted close to Marian, pressed up to her side, and didn't complain when Marian put her arm around her and squeezed.

"How've you gotten on, then? Your brother and sister

looking after you, or have you been marking all the trouble they've got into?"

Eleanor smiled, her face lighting up, as good as a laugh for her. Marian brushed a strand of sun-lightened hair out of her face.

The old wives round about said that Eleanor was a changeling, a queer unworldly thing, while the real child was stolen away by fae spirits. Punishment for her parents' wild ways. Or more charitably, the Fair Folk wanted a bit of the legend for themselves and so took their third baby and left something else in her place. Quiet, knowing, haunted. No one ever told the stories in Marian's hearing, but she knew. And knew they were wrong, even if she was the only one who looked in Eleanor's eyes and saw her father's spark there and Marian's own watchful manner. Eleanor did not speak but she listened, she knew, and she was their own girl.

And would Robin bargain his youngest daughter away if it suited him, even if she couldn't speak to say yes or no? No, that was where Marian would put her foot down.

If Eleanor didn't speak, it wasn't because she was changeling but because her siblings never let anyone get a word in edgewise. They were still at it, across the yard.

Robin scowled. "John, Mary, enough from both of you. There are no more outlaws in Sherwood."

Mary put in, "But—" then clamped her mouth shut.

Marian frowned; Robin caught her gaze across the courtyard, then looked away.

Perhaps, he should have said. Perhaps there were no more outlaws in Sherwood.

~

Something had shifted, gone off-balance. When the lord and lady returned, everything should have gotten back to the way it was. Mary expected some kind of calm to return. But a simmering wrongness lingered. Mother and Father were in the middle of an argument, which must have been going on some time, as unhappy as they both were. They pretended all was well but Mary caught them exchanging scowls.

While her mother was gone, Mary had taken on some of the responsibilities of the lady of the manor. She had made decisions about the cooking and cleaning; she had taken care of Eleanor and made sure she ate and that her clothes were mended. She had held Marian's keys for her. And now she gave them back and found herself at loose ends. But she didn't *want* those keys, that responsibility. She would not inherit this place; John would. His future wife would hold the keys, and what was there for her then? A flattering, horrifying marriage. Or a convent. She had overheard talk about Eleanor taking vows and becoming a nun—a vow of silence would not be so difficult for her, their father had joked, but Marian had glared and said that Eleanor could do whatever she liked and if she wanted to stay at Locksley and get underfoot her whole life, well, John would just have to put up with her. They hadn't said that about Mary.

Mary was as tall as her mother now, and she hadn't noticed that before the months they were gone.

That evening, they held something of a feast to celebrate Robin and Marian's return. They had brought gifts from London, a bit of silk and some spices from the Holy Land, and there were sweets and music. Robin told the story of facing King John and persuading him to the rightness of his cause. He was a good storyteller, expansive, his flattery becoming subtle mockery with a shift in tone. Her father walked a line between deference to the rightful King of England, a title and position he revered, and the old hatred of the man who now held that title.

It was exhausting. She picked at her food, picked at the seam in her kirtle, found herself slouching and tried to sit up straight, and wondered why she bothered.

A few days later, when the travelers had settled back into manor life, there was washing and mending to be done. Mary sat outside with her mother, sister, and some of the other women of the house. She wore a gown today, all proper, her hair neat and braided. And it wasn't that she minded all this, the baskets of cloth and yarn and chatter of women that sounded like starlings. But she would blink and find herself staring out at the road, hands resting in her lap with tunic and needle, mid-stitch.

Will was putting John through his paces with sword and buckler to see if the boy had practiced while they were gone. Wooden swords clacked as they parried one way, then the other. Will pressed John back, invited John to press him. John *had* practiced, his blocks and thrusts were surer than they had been at the start of summer. Will grinned and seemed pleased, while John frowned, serious and determined.

Mother was also watching them, her work resting in her lap, unmended. She seemed so very sad, and this made Mary uneasy. Lady Marian was the merriest person she knew, apart from Father.

Mary shook herself awake and tried to be attentive. "What did you like best about the king's court?" she asked her mother.

"Oh, the news, I think. News from abroad, from across the kingdom."

"Did you meet the queen?"

"Not really, not so as to mention." Marian winked and donned a bit of a grin. "Her Majesty mostly wanted a look at your father. But these days, he doesn't look so very much like the stories say he did. I think she was disappointed."

"Surely not," Mary said, astonished.

"Or it may be only that *everyone* was angry with your father. But no, I mostly stood to the side and watched with the rest of the wives. I'll tell you a secret, though: the wives have all the good gossip." A dog barked, ran up to Will and John, who stopped sparring to send it away, laughing. Mary was trying to think of what gossip Marian meant. Nearby, Joan and Beatrice were talking about which chickens were laying best this month and which might be ready for the soup pot.

"Why is Eleanor so much better at spinning than I am?" Mary said. Her sister had diligently spun her entire bundle of wool and started on the next.

"She doesn't get distracted."

Her sister seemed hypnotized by the spindle in her hand and the slender, perfectly even yarn twisting around as it emerged from between her small fingers. The stitches Mary had been making in the tunic seemed hideously large and uneven. Her mother would look at them and say, "It's fine, it's not like we'll be showing it to the king."

Father came around the corner then, dusting off his hands, appearing nothing like the nobleman he was, in a faded tunic, the sleeves rolled up, mended leggings and sweat-stained cap. He'd been looking over the livestock. He paused a moment to watch John and Will. But his smile fell when his gaze came to the women. Mother pointedly did not look back at him at all.

Then he called, "Mary, will you walk with me? Perhaps we can put a few arrows in a target. I fear I'm a bit out of practice."

This was flatly untrue, and this was odd. She glanced at her mother, who murmured, "Go on. He has something to tell you."

Even Eleanor looked up then, and Mary's stomach turned over.

She knotted the stitch she'd just made, broke the thread, put the tunic back in the basket, and went to meet her father.

He was pensive. She had watched for his glad smile or wicked smile and hadn't seen either one. Now he hardly looked at her as they took the path from the back of the manor, across the grassy stretch to the archery stand. Bales of straw stood at varying distances, with painted cloth pinned to them for targets. There was often someone out here practicing, either the children of the manor or Locksley's guards and foresters. Robin valued his archers. Today, the field was empty.

Robin squinted and looked across the quiet field. "I seem to have forgot my bow."

"Because you had no intention of shooting."

"And how has your practice been getting on? You've been practicing while we were gone, yes? I know many folk think a girl should not use a bow, but you're as good a shot as any man in the kingdom—"

Mary said, impatiently, "Mother said you have something to tell me."

He crossed his arms and finally looked at her. "While we were in Surrey, I met a young man. William de Ros. He's the son of the Baron of Helmsley, a good friend and ally. He will inherit."

The last bit of the description remained unspoken: *he's looking for a wife.* And perhaps Mary was no longer too young and this offer was not too grasping.

"Is it all arranged, then?" she asked. "I'm to marry him?"

"You don't miss a thing, do you? To think I was afraid I would have to explain it all, and that there would be tears. But no, it's not entirely arranged. We've got some time yet to think it over." He watched her, likely looking for some reaction, and she tried to think of what reaction to give him. She felt strangely distant from it all.

Finally, she asked, "Why is this offer better than the one you refused last year?"

He started. "You weren't supposed to know about that."

"Yes, but have you tried keeping secrets around here?"

He laughed, shook his head. "That man was twice your age and he's already put two young wives in their graves. He has six children, and yours would not inherit his land and titles. You'd have been an ornament to him, something to brag about. You would not have been safe."

"And I will be, with William de Ros?"

"I hope so."

Would any of them ever be safe? She had listened to the talk running through the manor: the charter Robin had won from the king would not be observed, war among the barons would come again, probably soon.

"If you need me to marry him, I will." There seemed to be precious little else she could do.

"Oh, no, *need* is a strong word. If you absolutely refuse, I will not press. Your mother would never speak to me again if I forced you to marry where you did not wish to."

"This is why she's angry with you?"

"She's furious with me for not asking you first. But . . . the offer came, and there wasn't time. You know, I never noticed this before but you're as tall as she is. When did that happen?"

"While you were gone, I suppose."

"Let's get back, shall we? We can talk more after you've had a chance to think about things."

They walked back together, and the world continued

to tilt off-balance. She expected him to kiss her cheek before he went back to his chores, as he'd always done when she was little. Instead, he gave an awkward dip of his head, something like a bow, and went off without a word. It made her sad.

This left her facing her mother, Eleanor, the women, and Mary found she didn't want to say anything at all.

"Well?" Marian asked. "You seem very calm."

"It's only that I don't know how else I should be right now. Did you meet this William de Ros?"

"Yes," her mother said, her voice carefully even.

"Is he tall?" What an odd thing to ask, but it was the first thing to come to mind.

"Not so much. But he is quite handsome. Earnest. Mary, you do not have to accept him if you do not wish it."

"But you think I should?"

"It doesn't matter what I think. Clearly." She muttered this last, studying the work in her hands with a scowl.

How much easier if they would simply tell her she must do this thing. Then she would know what she must prepare for. Or she could stay at Locksley forever and . . . what? She saw nothing clearly. She was an arrow in need of a bow, to send her off in one direction or another.

"If you'll excuse me, please." She needed to think. She needed to be alone, and so she fled. Her mother didn't call her back, and Eleanor watched her go.

In her room, she stared at her hands and wondered what they were good for. She had a callus from a needle and another from a bowstring. She didn't fit into her own skin, mostly because she wasn't sure what that skin was meant to do. It was all very confusing. She stripped out of her gown, put on her leggings and tunic and leather shoes, and left the house by the back way. If she marched with confidence, like she had a job to do, no one would stop her or question her. She looked like a stableboy, not the lord's daughter. She didn't know how much longer she'd be able to get away with the disguise.

Footsteps ran up the path behind her. "Where are you going?" John asked, coming alongside. And how had *he* found her?

"I'm just taking a walk," Mary said.

"May I come with you?" John asked, his manner so calm and polite, she couldn't refuse.

"I can't stop you," she said, sounding surly and childish to her own ears.

Before they'd even left the manor grounds, they passed Eleanor sitting on the fence of the paddock outside the stables, arms crossed. She seemed to study them both, her face pursed up with concentration.

"I suppose you want to go too?" Mary said.

Her sister hopped off the fence and walked up between them, and on. Mary and John exchanged a glance. He shrugged, as if to say he didn't understand her either.

So much for getting away from everyone and not having to talk.

The path went through a pasture, then through a barley field, and then it faded away. If they cut off in one direction they would come to the main road. But Mary went ahead, to the trees of Sherwood. The afternoon light shone golden, and the shadows among the oaks seemed not so dark. Mary wanted to climb into some branches and sit for a while. She didn't know if her siblings would understand. For now, she kept walking.

"What do you think really happened, when Father spoke to the king?" John said.

"Who's to say? Everything about Father is stories."

Eleanor ranged ahead, finding a stick and using it to turn over rocks and little hummocks of rotted leaves, looking for mushrooms. Mary almost told her not to eat anything she found, but she knew Eleanor knew better than that.

"Do you not think the stories are true, then? The old ones, I mean. About Mother and Father and Uncle Will and Much and the rest?"

Mary didn't answer. She wanted to believe them, but she didn't want to admit she did, which meant, really, she likely didn't believe them at all. Except . . . except she had met the ghost. Even now, she glanced up, searching the shadows between boughs and branches for a tall man wearing a hood.

Up ahead, Eleanor had straightened and now stood rigid, looking at something hidden among the trees. Mary saw it immediately and grabbed John's arm. She reached for her sister just as Eleanor backed into her grip.

Three, no four of them—men lurking within a dense copse. They might have been walking along just as innocently as the children, just as surprised by the appearance of anyone else in this corner of the forest. But they had bows and quivers on their shoulders, and swords at their belts.

"We should be getting home," Mary said calmly, to no one in particular, and guided her siblings back the way they'd come. "We'll be missed soon."

If the men had been there for some innocent reason, they would have let the children go. Mary, John, and Eleanor should have been able to simply walk away. But the men had a purpose, and without a word they rushed forward.

"Go, run," Mary said, pushing John and Eleanor behind her, putting herself between them and the attackers.

Three more men came out of the trees on either side of them, swords drawn. John tried to dodge, but one of them scooped him up and turned him upside down over his shoulder. John kicked and shouted but it did no good. Mary kept Eleanor behind her; her sister clung to her tunic. No matter which way she turned, there seemed to be more of them.

A cry came from above, a wolf-like howl that chilled her spine.

The ghost fell from a high oak, straight down on the first group of outlaws. His staff came down on one head, then another, then swept across the legs of the third. Shouting and panic followed. Mary took Eleanor's hand and ran, pausing only long enough to kick at the knee of the one who held John. The man howled and swung out a fist; Mary didn't duck fast enough and was sent sprawling. John cursed and raged; both he and his captor fell.

And then, the *thunk* of an arrow striking a target.

In terror, Mary looked for the sound, and saw the ghost fall to his knees, an arrow sticking in his right shoulder. His staff dropped; his arms hung loose. He looked at the wound as if he could not believe it, and chuckled.

She got her first real look at the Ghost of Sherwood. He was a tall, large man, incongruously large for the nimble way he climbed in and out of trees, for how silently he moved. He had shaggy hair, a grizzled beard, and his clothes were worn and patched.

Across the way, he met her gaze, and Mary saw such

sadness there, her breath caught. His shoulders slumped, as if he resigned himself to his fate. The men he'd attacked got to their feet; one of them kicked the ghost in the gut. His back arched in pain, and he cried out.

Another of the outlaws, a broad man with a ruddy beard, stalked to the ghost and grabbed his hair. "Who are you?"

"No one," he murmured.

Eleanor was kneeling by Mary, her eyes wide and filling with tears, her teeth gritted like she wanted very much to scream but couldn't.

Mary told her, "Run, run and get help!"

Her sister shook her head, quick and scared like a bird, and kept her grip on Mary's tunic. Before Mary could think of what else to do, one of the other men put an arm around Eleanor's middle and hauled her back. Another did the same to Mary, and she screamed, all fury now.

"Let go of her, keep your bloody hands off her, if you hurt her, I'll murder you, I'll murder you all!" She kicked and flailed—John was still doing likewise—until her captor put an arm across her throat and locked her head back until she could hardly breathe. Pinned now, she couldn't move.

The ruddy-bearded man turned to her. "And who are you? Some farmer's brats? Or something else?"

"She looks like Locksley's bitch," one of the others said.

John yelled, "How dare you! She doesn't kill you first, I will, we'll rip all your heads off—" Then he was cut off with a hand over his mouth, and they were all firmly caught.

"Do you belong to Locksley, then?" the broad man said, sounding pleased. He studied them and seemed to make some calculation. "What are the baron's children doing wandering off alone, hm? Outlawry runs in the blood, I think."

"We were supposed to take the woman," one of the others said. "The baron's lady."

"This is better."

"Locksley will murder us if we take his kids."

"On the contrary. We hold a knife to their throats, he'll do whatever we want. Our master can hold them hostage for years. Keep Locksley tame."

Their master—she thought of all the people who had a grudge against Father, all the names that came up when talk turned to politics. It could have been anyone. A name wasn't going to help her.

"Wait. Edmund, where'd the bloke go?"

"What bloke?" said the ruddy man.

"The man I shot, where is he?"

Mary craned her head and saw that the Ghost of Sherwood had disappeared, leaving behind only a mark of blood on the road.

"Christ, Morton. You two, go find him and slit his throat."

"I had my eyes right on him! He just disappeared!"

"No, he crawled away when you weren't looking—"

"They say Sherwood Forest is haunted. Maybe he wasn't—"

"Bollocks! Go find him, now!"

Someone else yanked her arms behind her and tied her wrists tight, then shoved a cloth in her mouth and tied it in place and slung her over a shoulder. She couldn't have done anything, she kept telling herself. There were too many of them and they were too strong.

And now the Ghost of Sherwood was likely dead, trying to save them. Mary choked back a scream.

They carried her and her siblings away, into the forest.

iv

DUSK CAME, AND MARIAN wasn't quite worried about the children yet. Eleanor had disappeared, but so had the other two, which meant they were likely together. Robin and Will were off visiting Much at the mill and smithy. When he returned, she'd ask if he'd seen them. They might have found each other on the way. She put away the mending and spinning, lit candles in the hall for supper, and added fuel to the hearth.

When an hostler rushed in from the yard, shouting, *then* she worried.

"My lady, there is a man at the gate. He's crazed, badly hurt—I would not let him in but he said . . . he asked for his lordship by name. He said the lord would see him. What should I do?"

"Show me," she said. They ran to the yard, to the gate, which stood open. A crowd had gathered and parted for Marian.

There, in the middle of the dirt path, Pol the stable master and one of his boys supported a man who had an arrow in his shoulder and was covered in blood.

"Take me to Robin. I must see him, please!" the man cried.

She was both shocked and not, to see this man before her after so many years. His beard grew to his chest, his hair stuck out wild, all of it gone to a kind of hoary gray, like frost on slate. The blood from the arrow wound was sticky, near dried. How far had he come seeking help, and who had done this?

He saw her at last, in the open space the crowd had made for her.

"Marian," he breathed. He lurched, and Pol and the boy stumbled to catch his weight.

Marian rushed up and displaced the boy to take his good arm over her shoulder, but he was too tall, too large, still all muscle and strength. She almost couldn't hold him. "Bring him into the hall. Send for Robin!" Pol helped her, and the boy ran off.

"I have news, I must tell you—"

"Tell us after we've got that arrow out and you've had a drink. God, John, what have you been doing?"

"The children, Marian. They are taken. I could not stop it."

She had been angry many times, she had been frightened many times, for herself and her friends and especially for Robin. But never like this, so that her breath choked in her throat and her blood ran to ice and she wanted to break something. No, she wanted a bow and arrow in her hand, and to kill something.

"Who? Who took them?"

They got him settled near the hearth, but the chill remained. Joan appeared with water and linen and a knife to cut off his shirt. John seemed dazed and hardly noticed.

"In the forest. Not outlaws. They had swords."

"And at least one of them was pretty good with a bow."

"No, I think he aimed for my head." He laughed, but softly. Not the old booming laugh. "I think . . . I think they were some lord's men. They followed orders."

"They could be outlaws, holding the children for ransom—"

He shook his head. "To threaten Robin. Where is Robin?"

"He'll be here soon."

"He won't want to see me . . ."

"But you came anyway." Someone handed Marian a cup of wine, which she offered to John. "Drink lots. We've got to get that arrow out."

"You must be out of practice, getting arrows out of stupid men."

"Not so much. Drink, John." Between her and Joan, they worked the arrow out, and John only groaned a little, keeping a tight grip on the edge of the chair. She had not seen Little John in sixteen years. Right after they learned of the death of Richard Lionheart. Right before Mary was born. He was right: she'd lost the knack of getting arrows out of stupid reckless men. This one had gone nearly all the way through, but it missed heart and lungs. If they could get the wound staunched and sewn up, it would heal.

When the arrow was out, she studied the bloody tip of it by the fire. It was slim, tapered to a graceful point.

"That's a bodkin point, my lady," Joan said softly.

Which meant the men who'd attacked John and her children were not hunters or outlaws taken unawares; they were armed for war. A lord's men, as he'd said.

He seemed to fall unconscious, then started awake again. "Robin, I must speak to Robin!"

"He's coming," she reassured him. He nodded, resting back against the chair.

There was a commotion, and now Robin stood at the front of the hall, staring as if he saw a ghost. "John. My God." Will and Much both came in behind him, wearing similar poleaxed expressions.

"Well met, m'lord," John said tiredly.

Marian finished putting stitches in the wound, and John was growing more alert after the drink, not less, as the pain dimmed. Good. He needed to explain himself. Robin rushed over, then hesitated, and Marian had never seen such a look of hurt and joy and confusion on him. She had never seen him speechless.

She said, "John, you must tell him about the children. Please. Robin, he says men took the children."

"I tried to stop them, but—" Marian laid a hand on his shoulder. Obviously, he tried to stop them. Did he think he could succeed against well-armed soldiers? Did he believe his own legends? "Seven men in the forest with swords and bows. They ambushed them, carried them all off. Mary and John made a go of fighting, but they were no match. And Eleanor—Mary told her to run but she would not leave them."

Marian's heart fluttered, and she nearly fainted. Dear, sweet Eleanor, what were they doing to her? Robin leaned on Marian's shoulder. His hand was shaking.

"They wore good armor and tunics, they were not outlaws," John said. "They went southwest, along the deer trail that runs near the road, where the stream branches near that stand of alders."

"Then we go," said Will, who was always the one to leap to action without plan or forethought or anything. He looked around, as if searching for a weapon, but there were none readily to hand. How the pattern went in the old days: Will would immediately demand some action, Much would advise caution, and Robin would laugh at them both and choose some middle, sensible road. And

John would follow Robin.

Now Much was silent, and Robin sank onto a bench, shaking his head.

"My enemies have done this. The king—I did not think he would bend so low, to take such revenge. I knew I had made enemies, but I did not think... I did not *think*. Marian, you were right. I should never have let them wander off, I should never have let them go off alone—"

As if he had had any say in the matter. "I never said that."

"They were always safe in the woods, Rob," John said. "I was always looking after them."

"I know," he said softly.

"I think in the old days, I would have been able to lay out all seven of them—"

"In the old days, you had all of us with you. No matter. We'll go after them now. They have brought their doom upon themselves. Will, Much, gather everyone you can, with every weapon to be had."

"Night is falling," Much said. "I'll get Giles. He's the best tracker we have."

"Yes, good. Send him ahead to catch them out. Will, you and I will follow and see what these scoundrels are made of—"

"And me, I'm going too," Marian said.

"Marian—" She gave Robin such a look that he drew back. "I think I may pity these fellows when you find them, my dear."

"We can make jokes later, when they're safe."

"Yes. Marian—" His voice caught, and she nearly burst into tears at that. Instead, she threw herself into his arms and clung there. He pressed his face against her neck, and they drew all the comfort they could from one another, their arguments forgotten.

In scant minutes they were ready, a troop of a dozen or so with weapons and shuttered lanterns, and strict instructions from Much to stay back until called. Still, it was too long, and Marian's thoughts kept slipping to what such men might do to children, and all to get at their father. She had changed into a tunic and leggings, pinned up her hair, donned an old wool hood. Looked just like a forester.

She returned to the hall to tell Robin it was time to go and found him sitting with Little John. The injured man was bundled with blankets, fast and warm, and finally seemed to be close to sleep. She might have told Robin to let him be, but they were speaking quietly. Smiling, as if no time had passed. And oh, please let this be a reconciliation between them. Robin was a stronger man with Little John beside him.

Quietly, she drew close and listened.

"Rob, why did you name the boy John? I understand why Mary and Eleanor. But why would you name the boy after that horrible man?"

Robin chuckled, and the sound came out harsh. "He's named for you, you brute."

John stared as if such a thing had never occurred to him. "Oh."

"Why did you never come home, my friend? You'd have been welcome any time. You should have come home."

"You should not have gone to Westminster." Robin gave him a look, and John ducked his gaze. "Sherwood is the only place I fit. The trees are bigger than I am."

Marian scuffed her feet to make a sound. "Robin, we're ready." She held his bow and quiver to him. He approached to take them from her, and in his gaze she saw both rage and delight. He had once made a career of revenge.

He marched out. John gazed longingly after.

"Stay there," Marian commanded. "Don't try to follow, you'll bleed out."

"Yes, my lady."

"We'll return shortly. And—thank you for looking after my children."

Little John grinned.

V

SOON ENOUGH, THEIR CAPTORS threw them down and made them walk, awkward and stumbling with their hands tied, choking on the gags. At least they hadn't gagged Eleanor, but then, she hadn't yet made a sound. Mary's sister tried staying close to her, but one of the men would come along and shove her apart, just for the sake of doing so, it seemed. They didn't travel very deep into the forest; they paralleled the road, even while keeping out of sight of it. Likely, they were meeting another party there. More enemies, more danger.

Finally, they stopped to rest. One of them kicked Mary's and John's feet out from under them, so they fell over. The men passed around water sacks but didn't move to let their prisoners drink.

The ruddy-bearded man, Edmund, stood before them and looked them over, scowling at John and Mary. He considered Eleanor further.

"You're a quiet one, aren't you? Not even a scream from you."

Eleanor stared at him, owl-like, in that disconcerting

way she had when she was unhappy.

"What's your name, then?"

Nothing. Mary's heart raced, knowing what would come next and being unable to stop it.

"I asked you your name, girl. What is it?" Eleanor was half his size—no, smaller even—but that didn't stop him from grabbing her face, squeezing, pushing until he shoved her against a tree. She didn't even squeak.

Mary did. She screamed, muffled against the gag, and thrashed against her bonds. Anything to get his attention. She choked herself on her own desperation. But the bully let Eleanor go, thank God.

Their captor came over and ripped out her gag. She spat against it, coughed. "She won't speak, she has no voice. Please, leave her alone, I beg you."

Edmund considered, glancing back at the girl who huddled by the tree, shivering. "No voice? Mute?" Mary nodded. "Is she simple?"

She didn't answer, because Eleanor was certainly not simple but she would seem so to a man like him. If they thought her so, maybe they would leave her alone. Or maybe they would torment her even more.

"What are your names?" the man asked her.

"I'm Mary. These are John and Eleanor." She hoped to set him a little at ease so he would stop harassing Eleanor.

He nodded. "Thank you, Mary of Locksley. Give them

some water." He gave this order to the youngest of them, a beardless youth with a constantly startled expression. He had a bruise on the side of his face—so he'd been one of the ones the ghost had struck. Alas, that the ghost hadn't killed them all.

And the ghost was likely dead now.

The young one came to them with a water sack and regarded John dubiously. "I take this off, you promise to be quiet?" John nodded quickly. They all stayed quiet and drank when he tipped the sack to their mouths. Eleanor spit the water back out. The boy sighed and left them alone.

Mary ought to keep quiet. She'd put Edmund somewhat at ease and ought to leave him there. But she didn't. "Who are you? Why are you doing this?"

"Your father has enemies."

She laughed. She didn't mean to; it was just such a ridiculous thing to say. Of course her father had enemies, but never ones that had stooped to kidnapping. "And is this meant to win him over? He will kill you for this."

He leered. "Not with you standing between us."

"Then you're a coward." She should not have said that. She expected that he would hit her for that, and she braced for it, determined not to cry out.

He stepped over to her and spoke low. "When I was a boy, I served the Sheriff of Nottingham. Many of my friends died with arrows in their backs. Robin of Locksley is the coward and should hang as a thief and a murderer. Taking you will remind him of what he has to lose."

"And you're so very brave and honorable, bullying young girls while they're tied up."

That time, he backhanded her with a closed fist. Her vision lit up; her skull rattled. She bent over, gasping. It hurt, and her nose filled. Blood, maybe. *Don't cry, don't cry . . .* Straightening, she stared at him, trying to project an utter lack of concern. She could pretend not to be frightened.

John's and Eleanor's eyes both went round; they stiffened with fear and anger. But they remained still and quiet. Good. If Mary could keep Edmund's attention, he would leave them alone.

One of the others laughed. "She certainly has her father's tongue, doesn't she?"

"Tell me, Mary of Locksley. You speak like your father. Do you also shoot like him?" He held up a bow. And what was he going to do now . . .

"Nobody in England shoots like Robin of Locksley," she said.

"But you do shoot?"

She nodded.

"I want to see."

He took a knife from his belt and cut the rope off her

hands. First thing she did was touch her face. Her right cheek was numb, and yes, her hand came away from her nose bloody. Gently as she could, she wiped her face with her sleeve. Made more of a mess than not, but nothing felt broken. Just bruised and bloody. Made it easier to glare at him. Slowly, she got to her feet.

He offered her a bow and arrow, and she took them, imagined shooting him. But he pointed off into the woods. "You see that birch there?"

It was far off, nothing more than a white line in shadow, especially in the late afternoon light. Edmund said, "If you can hit the notch between those two branches, I will let you all go."

She couldn't do it. It was too far away and he knew it. He was teasing her. But the worst part was John and Eleanor both looked at her with hope, as if they believed they were already saved.

He added, "And if you point that at any of us, I will beat the little one bloody. Do you understand?"

"Yes, sir."

"Now shoot."

Her eyes watered, trying to keep the target in sight. She blinked to clear her vision, breathed to steady herself. She must quiet her heart if she was going to be able to shoot at all, much less hit anything. Her face still throbbed and her limbs felt like ice. She shook her arms to loosen them. Planted her feet and tried to feel the earth under them, to root her down.

The bow wasn't the best—it hadn't been well cared for, and would likely split before too much more use. The arrow likewise—both had been made quickly, without much thought to quality. She ran her fingers over them, feeling their weaknesses, taking them into account. The draw was too heavy for her, but no matter; she only had to do this once.

She had been taught to shoot by the greatest archer in England. She imagined her father's hand on her shoulder, as he'd helped her when she was young. Stand like this, watch where your hips are, your shoulders—aim doesn't come from the arms alone, but from the whole body. Do not look at your hand, the bow. Look at the target and send your will there. Once you have drawn, do not force the shot—simply let go. Breathe out, release.

The whisper of air, the *thunk* of a target struck—the sounds of her childhood, when they practiced at the butts behind the manor, John with his first small bow, Eleanor in her basket, fussing and crying, when she still knew how to cry, and Mother and Father cheering when Mary hit a bull's-eye. Happy days.

She had closed her eyes, after releasing the arrow. She didn't want to look. Her arms fell to her sides. The glade was silent, so silent she thought she could hear the fletching on the arrow still trembling.

"She did it," one of them murmured. The youngest of them. Astonished, he looked at Edmund, then ran off to the birch. Raised a hand and confirmed, yes, well struck. The white line was interrupted—she had hit the notch, dead center. John laughed.

"Of course I did. I'm Robin Hood's daughter," she said, because it would make them furious to hear it.

The youngest of them returned with the arrow resting in his hands, staring at it. It might have been a holy relic, and a murmur went round the company, *Robin Hood, he's real.* Their gazes held wonder. Trepidation. A couple of them glanced over their shoulders, for what might be lurking in the woods. *Where is Robin Hood?* they whispered.

She was astonished and might have laughed at them for being foolish. But she was the one who said the name first, wasn't she? Invoked his name. Conjured him. She held herself straight and steady, holding the bow easily, as if it had been born in her hand. One of the outlaws of legend. Let them think that when they looked at her, as if she'd had any part at all to play in those stories.

"Well?" she asked, glancing back at Edmund.

Edmund's look darkened. He glared as if she had insulted him, and she waited for him to hit her again. But he only said, "I'm not letting you go."

"But—" John started to argue, then thought better of it.

Mary held on to the calm she'd claimed, to make that shot. "That's what I thought." She dropped the bow at his feet.

"Somebody tie her," Edmund said, and marched off. One of them did, her hands behind her back, harder and tighter than they needed to. Because they were afraid.

The party got John and Eleanor to their feet and continued on.

vi

WHEN THE NEWS CAME of King Richard's death, Marian, Robin, and his folk gathered in Robin's upstairs chamber, not by any plan but by a need for old comfort. These were the men and women who had lived in the greenwood with him until just a few years before, and they still felt the bonds of that time. Much leaned against a wall, his arms tightly crossed, his face puffed up and brave and tears sliding down his cheeks anyway. Will held his head bowed, his hands laced, apart from the others, outside the light of the hearth fire. Brother Tuck, clutching prayer beads, murmured. Tuck would be dead in ten years, but he lived long enough to christen all three children. Alan, Raymond, George, a half dozen others who'd followed Robin to Locksley manor and a lawful life. Grace, who cut her hair short and wore a tunic and leggings like a man and looked after the dairy cows, and who was as good an archer as any of the others. She stared at the fire, her face a mask. Bess had still been alive then and sat with Marian, fussing, because Marian was only weeks away from giving birth. She lay in a chair, bundled in fur, her feet propped up on cushions, sad and miserable and frightened. Robin stood by her, holding her hand, but his mind was elsewhere.

Little John came in last, quiver over his shoulder like he expected them to go into battle. "It's true, then?" He only had to look around the room and its weight of grief to know it was true. "Are we sure his death was natural? Not murder?" So many had wished for the death of Richard Lionheart.

"He died of a wound at Limousin in France," Robin answered. "I suppose, in a sense, one can call it murder. But all legal."

"And his brother will become king?"

Robin's voice was soft, resigned. "It was King Richard's will that it be so."

Agitated, John paced and swore enough to make Bess gasp. "Could he not have taken just a year or so off from his wars to father an heir? Anyone would be better than that . . . that . . ." He closed a fist and growled. "What are we to do?"

Robin squeezed Marian's hand, let go. She resisted reaching after him, and then the baby—Mary-to-be—kicked hard and she had to shift her weight yet again. Her husband went to the middle of the room, took up a martial stance as he had so many times, chin tipped up, resolved. Hopeful faces lifted to him. He had a plan, yes, and they would once again fight against the man who had done them so much harm—

"I will go to Westminster and swear fealty to the rightful King of England," Robin said.

The silence turned brittle. Marian watched the faces, mouths open, tears welling, turn from shock to anger to resignation, and the grief deepened. That they must call this man king. That Robin would not fight.

"You can't, Rob," John said simply.

"But I must. If I want to protect these lands and what we've built here—I must. I wish you all would go with me. He knows you by reputation if not by sight. It would send a powerful message."

Will was not the only one who grinned at the thought of what the new King John would do when confronted with Robin and his followers, now upright loyal subjects. He would turn green.

Most of these people would follow Robin into hell if he asked them.

"That man hates you, and you will bend a knee to him?" John said, disbelieving.

"There is power here. The king is only king as long as the barons support him, and I can use that. Ensure he never treats anyone the way he treated us."

"Us? You're a lord, and the rest of us are lowborn. There is no us. You choose your wealth and title over your honor," John spat.

Robin hated when John threw down their ranks. He glared. "Will you please listen—"

"I can't do it," John said. "I won't kneel before that man."

"Oh, John. I need you most of all. Marian, tell him what it means, why I must go—"

"You're both right, that's the devil of it." She shook her head. "When you turned outlaw, you had nothing to lose. Now . . . I at least have so very much to lose. Bess, help me, I need to walk a bit." Her maid took her arm and she lumbered to her feet like some bloated cow. Everyone, all Robin's followers, flinched as if to leap up and help her. Sometimes, she felt like a bit of heraldry, the flag they followed, some holy icon. Robin's lady. Ignoring them, she rested her hand on the ache in her back and walked slowly, balancing the baby's weight. Movement helped the little one settle, for now. "Robin's right. He can do more good behind the new king as a loyal baron than in front of him with a sword. But no one should have to bow to a man who treated them so ill." They didn't know it then, but the swords would come out again one day.

"If you go to kneel before him, he will find an excuse to hang you," John insisted.

"No, I think it will be the sword and block for me next time," Robin said, grinning.

"Robin, don't joke," Marian said, and his grin fell dead away. "If he harms Robin, he risks outright rebellion from the barons. Richard has nephews. There are other heirs if the lords and bishops of England back them. The new king knows this. He must placate his vassals. So, the Baron of Locksley has the power here, at least for now."

John chuckled bitterly. "I've never understood such power."

The power of reputation, of tit for tat, back-and-forth, and hope and fear? That was all the power women like her had ever had. But she lied. "Neither have I, but it's there nonetheless."

"Marian, are you well?" Robin asked gently.

"Stop asking me that, please." She should not snipe at him, but he had asked that every single day for the last five months, and God, she was tired. The baby kicked so powerfully, like she wanted to break out through the skin, and Marian was so frightened and angry at her helplessness and she hadn't told anyone that, not even Robin. He wouldn't have understood, would have tried to make it better with a joke, and he needed to ride to Westminster—"I loved King Richard like a father, but if he wished to be King of England, he perhaps should have spent more time ruling it and less fighting wars abroad. This is partly his fault."

Robin begged John. He never begged. "Come with me. Be one of my men. Just to see the look on his face when we stand before him together—"

"And then kneel? No. I cannot." John stood, took up his cloak and hood. "You must do what you will, and so will I. My lady." He made a quick awkward bow to Marian and turned to go.

"Where are you going?" Robin demanded.

"You take your fortune for granted, my friend," John replied. "Fare you well."

Some of the others called after him, but he marched out of the chamber, then out of the manor, and that was the last time any of them had seen Little John.

In the years since then, she often looked up in the trees, studied the shadows for a hooded figure who might linger there. Several times a year, she went to one of the springs and left a basket with new stockings, a wool blanket, some sausages and cheese and the like. Odds and ends that might be useful to someone living in the greenwood. Others of their folk did likewise, she knew. The baskets always came back empty, hanging from a branch at the edge of the woods near the manor. She wished for a way to ask him to come home. Robin rarely spoke of him, but she caught him searching the shadows, too. Now and then, a forester would come and tell of snares he'd found, someone poaching rabbits in Sherwood—and Robin would say to let it go, never mind. It was only a few rabbits.

And now John Little was back. No—he had always been here. Sherwood had always been haunted.

vii

NIGHT FELL, AND THEY had not left the forest or reached any kind of destination. Their captors made a camp some ways into Sherwood, near a spring that they probably thought no one else knew about. They started a small fire burning, though some of them grumbled about it.

"No one will find us here, and it's too cold to go without," Edmund said. So the fire stayed lit.

They set her and John and Eleanor up against the trunk of an oak, all in a row. At least they were together. Eleanor leaned against Mary; she was shivering. Mary wished she could put an arm around her, but she could only lean her head against Eleanor's and give her a quick kiss.

"Father will come looking for us," John said decisively.

"Will he?" Mary whispered. "They may not even know we're taken, and these men will meet with horses on the road and carry us away. How will Father find us then?"

"But he will. He must."

"We must find a way to escape."

"How?"

One of the men spoke. "I don't like this, Edmund. Nothing's gone right, and it's dangerous, staying the night here."

"There's nothing here can harm us."

"There's Robin Hood."

There it was, an icy stillness, a stab of fear. The men glanced into the darkness among the trees, and fists squeezed on the grips of swords.

"Robin Hood is a myth," Edmund said, scowling. "There were only ever thieves and cowards here. Robin of Locksley is an old man who can't stop us." But Robin of Locksley was Robin Hood; he all but admitted it, speaking both names together. Edmund's men were not set at ease.

"That man who fell out of the trees—who was he, then?"

"Just some outlaw—"

"What if it was one of Robin Hood's men? What if he's gone to get others—"

"And if you'd bloody found him and cut his throat like you were supposed to, we'd know he hadn't! He's bled out in a ditch by now. He's nobody."

Mary looked at John out of the corner of her eye, and he was looking back at her, jaw set and eyes blazing. And on her other side, Eleanor—Eleanor was undoing the knots in the rope around her hands. Slipping right out of the bindings by some magical process. Maybe they hadn't bothered binding her very tightly; after all, she was only a little girl. But no, she was simply *escaping*. As Mother had said, Eleanor didn't get distracted.

Mary spoke very softly. "Get help. Follow the stream back to the mill and find Uncle Much, get help."

Eleanor shook her head, glanced at the ruffians for a moment, and smiled a familiar, wicked smile.

Mary held her breath. Eleanor had always done exactly as she wished in the end. "Be careful."

Eleanor dropped the ropes and crept behind the oak, into the dark.

"What's she doing?" John whispered.

"Shh." They couldn't talk. They couldn't draw attention. Eleanor had a plan, God knew what and how stupid it would be. The men would notice she was gone sooner rather than later, and she needed to be well away—

Unless they didn't notice. Bow and arrow had never been their father's only weapon.

Bracing her shoulder against the trunk, Mary got her feet under her and levered herself to standing. Took some doing, with her hands bound, but she managed to stand straight, as if she had some measure of control.

"Hey there, what're you doing?" one of the men called, and the rest looked.

"You're risking much, making your camp here," she said. "These woods are haunted."

"Then why aren't you afraid?" Edmund asked, chuckling.

"Sherwood knows who we are. It knows our blood, and we have its sap in our bones. *We're* safe." She smiled. Her father's wicked smile. "But you're outsiders, and you know the stories."

A silent moment followed; the fire crackled, popped.

Edmund laughed nervously. "Silly brat, thinking you can frighten us."

She went on; she couldn't not. "You should be frightened."

Happily, wonderfully, a fox cried, a sound like a man being strangled. One of the men gasped; they all jumped, even Edmund. This drove him to a rage, and he marched across the camp and grabbed her by the throat to pin her against the tree. It happened so quickly, she hardly knew what to think, just that her vision swam and her breath suddenly stopped up.

John shouted a defense, tried to throw himself bodily at their attacker, who simply kicked him away.

Edmund's smiling voice held a vicious edge. "You're a pretty one under all that provincial dirt, aren't you? Maybe we could sell you off. Marry you to some loyal baron's son, keep you under our thumb that way, hm?"

She would spit at him but her mouth was too dry and she couldn't seem to catch her breath.

"You will sit still," he said, pressing harder, and she was choking. "You will be quiet and accept your fate. Your father cannot save you."

"What's that!" one of the men called, and others rushed to the edge of the camp to peer into the darkness where, deep in the woods, a light was burning. A small flame, like witchlight. No telling what it was or what it meant. It might have been a torch, but it did not move, glaring like an eye. A small orange light, as if the forest itself had lit a candle.

And then another appeared, some distance on. Then another—in about the time it would take for a young girl to move from one spot to the next, but the men didn't think of that. Eleanor, silently and without fuss, had snuck close enough to steal a brand from the fire.

It seemed as if the camp was being surrounded by witchlights.

"I warned you," Mary said, coughing. Her throat was bruised, and her breath came rough. It made her sound fierce, and she said, more boldly, "Sherwood protects its own. It always has. Those who've wronged Robin Hood never escape its shadows."

Edmund slapped two of his men on the shoulders. "You, go see what it is. It's some trick. Peasants with lanterns. Take your swords and run them through!"

"But it's Robin Hood's outlaws!"

"It isn't! Go kill them!"

Mary closed her eyes a moment and made a prayer for Eleanor to stay quick, stay silent. Now she must run and get help, yes?

Something, likely a small stone, struck the younger of the brutes on the head. Then another. The man fell moaning, hand clasped to his forehead, probably from surprise rather than pain. There wasn't even any blood that Mary could see, but he acted as if he'd been sliced by an ax.

"Oh God, what is it!"

Another stone flew and struck the next man, who stumbled to his knees.

All Robin's children inherited his smile, and his aim.

"Elfshot! The ghosts of Sherwood strike, these woods are haunted!"

"Nonsense! It's a trick. Get out and see who's out there!"

"I can't see anything!"

"Put the fire out, they can find us!"

"They've already found us, you idiot!"

Mary called, "The ghosts have come for you, and you cannot stop them."

The young one with the astonished expression

screamed and ran from the camp, into the woods, his cries echoing. Edmund hollered after him but only inspired one of the others to drop his sword and run too.

Mary watched, marveling. John had got to his feet. He had a big red bruise on the side of his face where Edmund had kicked him, but he was smiling.

Then something small and soft touched Mary—her sister's hand, holding hers. A pull and a push—and the knots binding her came loose. A shadow behind her moved, and Eleanor, wide-eyed and serious, looked back.

Everyone in the camp was yelling at each other, drawing their swords, or aiming their bows and arrows at darkness.

"We've got to get out of here," John said, stating the obvious but full of nerves, shaking ropes off his hands with an air of disgust after Eleanor untied him.

"If we run, they'll chase us," Mary said. She glanced up.

John looked where she did and grinned. "But if we disappear, they'll fear us. Get me up first and I'll pull up Eleanor." Mary, he knew, could climb on her own. She made a step with her hands, John put his foot there, and she lifted as high as she could. He straddled the wide branch just above their heads and reached for Eleanor, who raised her arms to him. Mary climbed, and in just a few moments, they were all in the oak and climbing higher, to the uppermost branches and well out of sight. Which meant they got to watch the rest of it.

It was the leader, Edmund, who noticed the children were gone. "You idiots! Go and look for them! They can't have gone far."

"The ghosts have taken them!"

Edmund was florid and screaming. "There are no ghosts! There is no—"

And then an arrow split the air and struck Edmund's neck.

~

Quickly, silently, Marian, Robin, and Will moved through the forest, looking for some trail to follow, some sign that a group of armed men had passed. Weren't too many places such a group could hide, and Little John had set them on the right track. Marian kept the lantern low and shuttered. The moon gave enough light to see by here.

Giles had been all but a child when he'd run with Robin's outlaws. Now he had a child of his own and worked for Locksley as a forester. He'd kept up his woodcraft, and Marian was pleased with Robin for recognizing that he'd gone a bit soft and would do better with a guide.

Near midnight, Giles returned to report on their prey. "Seven of them, as John said. They've made a camp. They seem sure of themselves, which makes me think they might be meeting others come morning."

"No doubt. And the children?"

"Alive," Giles said with a firm nod. "But they've taken blows."

"I will kill them all," Robin said.

"Yes, my lord." Giles' eyes lit at the prospect. He pointed the way to go, then continued back to bring news to Much and his troop.

And then the kidnappers came to them.

It was an odd thing. A human scream of terror echoed, followed by the sound of crashing, of branches breaking and a body falling, picking itself up, falling again. Robin gestured, and Will and Marian spread out to wait.

A young man plunged around shrubs and trees, screaming like a pig, and stumbled to his knees when confronted with the three figures, two of whom held arrows nocked.

He drew back, his face in a rictus, as if demons of hell had appeared before him.

"Who are you?" Will called.

Then, strangely, the terrified man laughed. "You are mortal men! Oh, God be praised, you must help me!" Robin lifted his bow, and the look of horror returned.

"You're him! It's true, you've come to kill us all! Oh, God have mercy, please have mercy, I didn't know, I didn't know!" He wept like a child.

"What's got into him?" Will asked.

"I will shoot him just to silence him," Robin muttered.

Marian approached, lifting the lantern and opening its light just enough to show her face so that she would appear as a vision in the dark woods. Smiled sweetly. He would think an angel spoke to him.

"Do you know where the children are?" she asked softly. "The children you took?"

His attention caught, he gazed on her, and his look of wonder turned to anguish. "Oh, Holy Mary in Heaven forgive me, please forgive me, I didn't know!" He clasped his hands in prayer, his whole body shaking.

"Well, that's something," Robin said, baffled.

The man went on. "Do not make me go back to the woods, do not make me go!"

"Something has happened," Marian murmured, looking ahead to the darkness, to the forest's secret depths. The old instincts came back quickly and she ran, without need of light, ducking branches, taking quick and careful steps among roots and moss.

"Marian!" Robin called after her, but there was no time.

Soon enough, she could tell exactly where the kidnappers were, because of all the shouting.

A spring formed a pool, a place where deer watered in the mornings. The men made camp around it, but now the lot of them were in chaos, shouting at each other, pointing out to the woods where faint torches burned. John had said there were seven, but Marian only counted four—five, with the young man who had run into them headlong. Robin and Will finally came up next to her.

"We trussed the poor lad up," Will said. "We'll have to remember to go back for him. Or not."

"I don't see the children," Marian murmured.

Robin held his bow, white-knuckled. "I know that man." He nodded to the one with the ruddy beard who harangued the others to get their wits about them, there were no ghosts in Sherwood, it was all a trick—

Robin drew his bow and let the arrow fly.

In the next breath, the stout man with the ruddy beard was dead on the ground, and his remaining men lost their minds. Will's arrow struck the next, and Robin's second arrow the next after that. By then, the fourth man was running deep into the woods—the wrong way from the road. With any luck, he would lose his way and die of thirst and hunger. Not many could make their livings in Sherwood, and none who could would help him. They let him go.

In the now-silent camp, there was no sign of the children. The fire burned low, throwing a glowering orange light and making the shadows of the trees dance like living things. Some distance away, torches burned—no, they were tufts of grass and moss, lit quickly and burning out. Distractions, Marian realized. But to strangers in Sherwood, they must have seemed like curses.

Robin kicked the body of the ruddy-bearded man. "He's one of the younger William Marshal's men." The elder William Marshal had remained loyal to the king, but his son had been with the rebels—for a time. Now, he must have thought he could prove his loyalty by taking hostages. What better way to control Robin of Locksley than by holding blades to the throats of his children? Robin raged. "*This* is how the braggart seeks favor with the king? By stealing children?"

"So, it wasn't the king's command that did this?" Marian asked.

"No," Robin admitted tiredly. "No, this time, the king has left us alone."

Will considered a moment. "We were perhaps a bit hasty killing them. If they've hidden the children somewhere—"

"Where in God's name are they?" Robin stormed around the camp, looking behind trees, turning over a cloak or two as if they might have been stashed there.

Marian saw the bits of ropes on the ground at the base

of a wide oak. She raised the lantern, looked up. Three pairs of shining eyes were tucked away high in the tree as if they had been born there, forest creatures well at home.

"Robin."

"What? Marian, my God, how can you be so calm?"

"Robin. Look up."

He and Will did, saw the children perched in the branches, gazing back calmly. Will laughed, and Robin bowed his head and aged a dozen years before her eyes.

As if they had come to the woods for a lark, Mary called, "We need help getting Eleanor down, please."

viii

THEIR FATHER CLAMBERED EASILY into the tree, though it must have been years since he'd done anything like it. Between them, Mary and John coaxed their sister to the next branch down to meet him. Keeping tight hold of her hand, Mary lowered her to their father's arms. Eleanor clung to him.

"Darling girl," he murmured against her head. "Were you very frightened?" She nodded solemnly, and Robin held her for a long, consoling moment. He in turn lowered her to Will and Marian, who gasped a little when she finally had the girl in her arms.

John was next, and he mostly made the climb himself but wasn't too proud to grab his father's arms when they came in reach.

"I was only a little frightened," John announced. "I knew you would come for us."

Robin laughed and cupped his son's face. "Good lad. Off you go to your mother, now."

Then came Mary. She sat on the branch just above her father's reach, waiting until Robin saw John safely down.

Thinking of what she would say when he looked back up at her. She might scream at him, as if this was all his fault. She might burst into tears like a child. She might do neither. Her face must have looked frightful. She saw that in his troubled gaze, however much false brightness his smile held.

"And what about you, Mary? Did you know I would come for you?"

"I knew you would try."

His expression fell, and she had a brief glimpse of an old man, full of care. "Oh, my sweet girl, I am so sorry."

She made her way to the next branch, putting herself on a level with him. "I was frightened for John and Eleanor. If they got hurt ... I couldn't let them get hurt. But I didn't know if I could stop it. That was what frightened me."

"That is a fear I know well." He reached out and brushed tears from her face. They had slipped silently, and her cold and aching cheeks stung with them. "There is no shame in fear. It's what keeps you and yours alive."

"Have you ever been afraid, really?" she said.

"This night, I was terrified."

Mary decided to be a child then, just for a moment, and she put her arms around her father's neck and cried while he held her.

They all arrived on the ground, and Marian came to

her, closing her arms around her, crying silently. "I'm all right, Mother. We're all right," Mary repeated, but found herself clinging. For as long as the night felt, the end of it had happened so quickly that part of her was still praying that their captors would leave Eleanor alone, and thinking of what to say next to the big bearded man to distract him from her siblings.

Even Will had to touch their shoulders and ruffle their hair, and Mary repeated that they were all safe. Eleanor wouldn't let go of Marian's arm, which was all right because Marian wouldn't let go of hers. Robin studied their wounds. In the dark of the oak, he hadn't seen their faces clearly, but in the firelight, the blood and bruises shone plain. John's eye was swelling shut, though he insisted it didn't hurt a whit. He was lying, of course. Then her father acknowledged the blood on Mary's face and tipped her chin up to see her neck. She wished she could see what he saw, then she didn't.

"Does it hurt?" he asked. He brushed the skin with a thumb and the bruises lit with pain. She winced and hissed. Robin had never looked so angry. "I can see the marks of a man's fingers there. Which one of them did this to you?"

"Him." She nodded at the one with the ruddy hair. He lay on his back, the arrow sticking straight up from his neck. His eyes had frozen wide. The firelight made the pool of blood under him shine. He'd been facing his death straight on and not seen it coming. Well, she'd warned him, hadn't she?

Marian had turned to block Eleanor's view of the dead men, though the girl kept trying to stare. "Don't look at them, sweetling," Marian murmured, and Eleanor pressed her face to her mother's arm. Mary couldn't not look. Same with John. They had seen the dead before, but this was different. The violence of it blasted like a lightning strike. Edmund still seemed about to shout at them. Mary wondered if she would have nightmares about this and felt a sudden need to practice her archery more diligently.

Robin glanced at Marian. "Can we bring him back to life and kill him over again? Slower this time."

"No, love. We will go back home, sit by the hearth and get warm, and tell Little John that all is well."

"Little John?" the younger John said. "What do you mean? He's real?"

Will glanced away and laughed, and Robin—well, the look on her father's face defied understanding.

"The Ghost of Sherwood," Mary said. "Didn't you ever see the hooded figure hiding in the trees?"

Her brother's brow furrowed. "Yes. But, well . . . I always thought I imagined it. He looked like something from the old stories."

Mary turned to her mother. "He's alive? We saw him shot, and he fell—"

"He'll be a long time healing. But yes, he's well, and will be relieved to see you all home safe."

Mary started crying again and quickly brushed the tears away.

"This is quite the mess," Robin said, regarding the three bodies. Will went to one, started to put his foot on it to yank out the arrow, when Robin held up a hand. "Leave them. We'll load them on a cart and send them to the Earl of Pembroke's son with Robin Hood's arrows sticking out of them. Let him make of it what he will."

Will gave a curt laugh. "That'll start a row."

"I'm not starting this one, am I? I never *started* anything, but by God, I will finish—"

Marian took Robin's arm, standing firmly between both him and Eleanor. "Robin, you have nothing to justify."

"Oh, no, it's just . . . I thought I could stop fighting." He touched Eleanor's cheek and kissed Marian.

Much and his troop arrived with horses to load the bodies on, and, by torch and lantern light, they started back for home. The younger of Edmund's men was some distance down the path—he had fled, screaming, and now he was tied up, and still screaming. Robin hauled him to his feet and wrapped his hands in the man's collar.

"No, please! I beg you, have mercy, have mercy!"

"Mary, did this one lay a hand on any of you?" her father asked. The man wept harder.

"No, he didn't," she said, though the curiosity of what her father would do if she said yes tempted her to lie. The power of holding this man's life in her hands was shockingly enticing.

"Well then. You are spared."

"Oh, thank you, God bless you, God bless—"

"You will take your fellows back to your master and tell him what happened here. Do you understand?" Sobbing, nothing more. Disgusted, Robin dropped him and let the others load him up with the dead bodies, which did nothing to settle the man's wailing.

Robin looked at his children. "What in God's name did you *do* to these men?"

Mary started to speak, then closed her mouth because she didn't know where to start. Didn't know how to tell what had happened without making it sound fanciful.

John answered him. "Mary told them that Sherwood is full of ghosts and looks after its own, and she was right."

The father regarded them, nonplussed. "Is that so?" John nodded, so sure.

"Those old stories are good for something after all," Marian said evenly. "Come along. I think dawn is nigh."

Indeed it was, and when they arrived back at the

manor, the sun was up. Mary was first in the hall, rushing in to see the ghost for herself: asleep, wrapped in blankets and furs, his naked shoulder bandaged. Entirely mortal, and this was a relief.

"He's asleep?" she whispered to Joan, who was seated nearby, with her spindle. The matron beamed at her, at them all when they came into the hall after her.

"Yes, my lady. He's had a long night but he's doing well. And you're safe? Everyone's safe?" All was well, all was safe.

The man, Little John, stirred. He squinted, focused on Mary, then sank back.

"God be praised," he murmured.

"Is he here?" the younger John called, running up next to Mary, and Eleanor was right behind him, until they were all lined up and staring at the Ghost of Sherwood.

"You're all here," Little John said wonderingly.

Mary sat on a bench nearby. "Why did you hide? Why not come out of the woods, even to visit?"

"Right at the moment, I can't think why. But I'm glad I was out there last night."

"Me as well. Thank you."

"The company of Robin of Locksley watches out for each other." He looked up to see Robin and Marian arrive, and chuckled.

They stayed in the hall while Joan fetched food and

wine, and they told the story of all that had passed. John—Young John, as they had begun to call him—told it best, though he stretched the truth almost to the point of breaking, going on about how he wanted to fight them all and steal their bows and put arrows in all their throats but Mary stopped him because she said the bows were too big for Eleanor to draw, and, and . . .

"You could have given Eleanor one of the swords," Robin said.

"Well, yes, that's true, but there were plenty of knives to be had, and that would perhaps be better."

"Oh, certainly."

"Dearest, don't encourage him," Marian said.

"Who, me? I never." Robin winked.

Mary decided then that she believed all the stories about her parents, every single one of them.

John continued. "Then the brute made Mary shoot a bow, to see if she could shoot like you."

"How did she do?" Robin asked, eyeing Mary across the hearth.

"The shot was impossible, but she did it. I don't think you could have done it, Father, but she did."

Robin laughed. "Well done, Mary."

"John, you're exaggerating," Mary said.

"I think we've earned some exaggeration, after this night," the boy said. "We spread this story, no one will ever bother us again."

"He isn't wrong," Will Scarlet said.

"Indeed," Robin said, and seemed pleased.

Then Robin and Will went out to prepare the cart and bodies to send to the Earl of Pembroke and his son; Little John fell asleep, and so did Young John and Eleanor. Eleanor slept with her head in Marian's lap, Marian's arm resting over her like a shield. John had wrapped himself in a blanket and settled on a bench. He shifted, restless.

Mary couldn't sleep. She'd watched Edmund and the others die and still couldn't entirely believe they were gone. She wasn't sure what she thought of her father's plan to send the bodies to the Earl of Pembroke—Mary had heard of William Marshal, and she wondered if he would send men back to Locksley, to attack in retribution for the deaths. Or if this would all be laid on the younger William Marshal and forgotten. It would never end. And Robin believed he could keep them safe.

"Mary?"

"Hm?"

"Just seeing if you're awake. You know, dear one, you don't have to marry William de Ros or anyone else if you don't want to."

She hadn't been thinking of marriage plans at all. Or maybe she had, without realizing it. Would marriage keep her safe? She looked at her mother's overtired face, the way her hand clenched protectively on Eleanor's arm and her gaze kept falling on John, the large man with the arrow wound who had been prepared to die for them, and Mary believed that no, it couldn't. But having good friends around you could.

"I think I would like to meet him first, before I decide."

"That would be wise."

"What do you suppose he'll make of a girl who can shoot better than he can?"

"I think in your case, he will expect nothing less."

Mary shifted seats, came to sit on the bench by her mother, being careful not to disturb Eleanor, and put her head on Marian's shoulder to try to sleep a little.

About the Author

Photograph by Helen Sittig

CARRIE VAUGHN'S work includes the Philip K. Dick Award–winning novel *Bannerless,* the *New York Times* bestselling Kitty Norville urban fantasy series, and more than twenty novels and upward of one hundred short stories, two of which have been finalists for the Hugo Award. Her most recent work includes a Kitty spin-off collection, *The Immortal Conquistador.* She's a contributor to the Wild Cards series of shared-world superhero books edited by George R. R. Martin and a graduate of the Odyssey Writing Workshop. An Air Force brat, she survived her nomadic childhood and managed to put down roots in Boulder, Colorado. Visit her at www.carrievaughn.com.

TOR·COM

Science fiction. Fantasy. The universe.

And related subjects.

*

More than just a publisher's website, *Tor.com*
is a venue for **original fiction, comics,** and
discussion of the entire field of SF and fantasy,
in all media and from all sources. Visit our site
today—and join the conversation yourself.